Indie Bites

Monsters & Masquerades

Issue 6: May 2022

A note on language

We are a UK publication, but we accept work from authors all over the world. We retain each author's version of English as written, so pieces from US authors appear in US English and pieces from UK authors appear in British English etc.

Published under licence by Silver Sun Books.

Table of Contents

Letter from the Editor 3

Interview with H.L. Macfarlane 7

Short Fiction 13

Glorious Monsters by D.N. Bryn 15

Lead Me Not Into Temptation by Josie Jaffrey 37

My Granny, The Dragon by Gemma Church 59

Behind You by Kristen Brand 71

The True Tale of the Sockburn Worm by Nova Warner 85

Reviews 93

Succulents and Spells by Andi C. Buchanan 95

A Fate of Wrath and Flame by K.A. Tucker 101

Letter from the Editor

This quarter's issue is all about monsters and masquerades. If you're enchanted by mysterious ballrooms and alluring strangers, or by dark mysteries and family secrets, then there's sure to be a story in this issue that you will love.

The monsters you're about to meet are a wonderful hodgepodge of seductive manipulators, terrifying wild beasts and beloved family members. Some of the stories are straightforward: the monster must be vanquished. Some are subversive: the monster is not a monster at all, so there is nothing to fight. And some, in fact the majority of the stories in this issue, will have you wondering who's the real monster anyway.

I love the kind of stories that make you question who's playing the villain and who's playing the hero. We all love a good twist, a little authorial sleight-of-hand that sets one character up as a demon, only to unmask them layer by layer to reveal the hidden depths beneath their facade. Combine that with the romance of a masked encounter – where identities are hidden and only the twinkle of an eye is visible to evidence a character's intentions – and I am hooked. I think you will be too.

Amongst the stories that follow, you'll find a vampire romance set during a masquerade ball, a dark tragedy of a love triangle and a little light relief from a tavern braggart who wants you to believe he's slain a mighty foe. We're also bringing you an interview with indie author and publisher H.L. Macfarlane and two reviews of indie novels from our review team, all on the theme of *Monsters & Masquerades*.

So let's get unmasked. There's plenty here to sink your teeth into.

Josie Jaffrey
Anthology Editor

Next quarter's issue is *Revenants & Renegades*, and submissions are open now. Submissions are also now open for our November issue, *Enchanters & Experiments*. If you're an indie author or illustrator who'd like to contribute to one of our upcoming issues, then check out our submissions page on our website. We'd love to have you on board.

This issue's cover image was created by Kristen Brand, a speculative fiction author who dabbles in photo manipulation art. She drops a new downloadable fantasy wallpaper every month at: TheShadowJournals.com.

A note on language: We are a UK publication, but we accept work from authors all over the world. We retain each author's version of English as written, so pieces from US authors appear in US English and pieces from UK authors appear in British English etc.

Meet Author H.L. Macfarlane

H.L. Macfarlane hails from Balmaha by Loch Lomond in Scotland. After studying for eight years at the University of Glasgow and obtaining a BSc (Hons) in genetics and a PhD in synthetic biology, Hayley hung up her lab coat for good and took up a pen. Throughout the process of writing and then publishing her own books she grew to love the publishing industry as a whole, and decided to become a publisher for other people's stories as well as her own. Alongside writing and publishing, Hayley also designs book covers, takes on art commissions and ghostwrites. Where does she find the time?! Nobody knows…not even her.

Welcome to Indie Bites! This issue we're exploring monsters and masquerades, so tell us – what kinds of monsters lurk in your work?

I love monsters in all shapes and sizes, but I especially love monsters in stories when they force us to look at our own humanity. Some of my books have very literal monsters – *Invisible Monsters* (no surprise) and the Bright Spear trilogy being prime examples – but other times the monster is more subtle, such as in *The Boy from the Sea.* Even when I'm being subtle, though, I like to refer back to well-known mythologies or parables about monsters so that the story still has that monstrous-folksy feel. The primary monster in *Invisible Monsters* is a satyr, which I had lots of fun with because you don't often find them in modern stories, and especially not as a villain.

If you were heading to a magical masquerade, what would your perfect costume be?

Oh ho ho ho, as a die-hard *Labyrinth* fan I've been dying to write a masquerade into my work. The second book of the Bright Spear trilogy, *Lord of Horses*, features an Unseelie Winter Solstice revel, which has all the vibes of the *Labyrinth* masquerade ball but none of the masks. I've gone to a masquerade party before, actually. I made moon and sun-themed masks for me and a friend, so I was dressed all in midnight blue and silver and she was rose pink and gold. But it wasn't a true *ball*, so I didn't get to dress as outlandishly fairy tale as I would have liked. My perfect costume would be a dress with a fitted bodice, low back and then a long and floaty skirt that's probably full of feathers (thanks Jareth and Howl for the feather obsession). I'd get bored of holding a mask on a stick so I'd want one that I can attach to my head/hair. I'd want big, curly goat horns on the mask probably, even though they wouldn't go with feathers… and lots and lots of dangly jewellery!

As well as publishing your own work, you run an indie publishing company too, Macfarlane Lantern Publishing. What does your typical publishing process look like?

Originally I wanted to publish full-length novels from promising authors with my indie publishing house, but that's too much work for one person to do alongside being a writer, ghostwriter, cover designer and artist (I make all my own book covers and marketing materials, and only work with one editor for my books, so it's very time-intensive!). So I'm focusing on anthologies, instead, because that allows me to promote a larger group of promising writers to the world whilst making the entire process easier for me to fit into my current workload.

For *Once Upon a Winter*, the first anthology I published last November, I put out an open call for submissions on Twitter. I think I got about 50 or so submissions within a couple of days! I whittled this down to around 15 writers and got a Discord group set up for them, where we discussed the specifics for the theme of the anthology, story lengths etc. etc. until everyone was happy with what we were doing and it fit what I wanted to do with Macfarlane Lantern Publishing. Then I got to work on the cover and marketing materials, and set up the ebook pre-order whilst I was still editing the stories. Once I had a final page count the paperback pre-order was put up, and myself and the authors all went very hard on the marketing front (thanks everyone!).

When the book came out I hosted a series of Instagram Live sessions with the authors so our audience could find out a bit more about everyone involved. I'm in Scotland so I had a huge time difference with some of the authors, resulting in one of the IG Lives being held at around 11pm. That was fun! There are four seasonal anthologies planned in the *Once Upon A...* series, and with the next one I've learned from all the teething problems with *Winter* to make the process more streamlined… I hope!

What's a monster you've always wanted to write about but have never had the chance to tackle?

I really love Celtic lore so I want to write about a selkie in the future, or a freshwater mermaid. A kelpie features prominently in the Bright Spear trilogy, and a satyr features in *Invisible Monsters*, and those were definitely the two I wanted to write about first and foremost. Their stories aren't over yet so other creatures will have to wait until then!

Which indie fantasy authors are you enjoying at the moment?

Rebecca F Kenney and Carol Beth Anderson are always my go-to indie fantasy authors! They're definitely both worth checking out.

What are you working on at the moment?

I'm working on the two sequel books to *Invisible Monsters* – *Insatiable Monsters* and *Invincible Monsters* – to release them in October 2022 and spring 2023. After that it's the Dark Spear duology, which is the sequel to the Bright Spear trilogy but set 200 years later. There's also the next of the *Once Upon A...* anthologies to put together! Before all of those, though, my very first contemporary rom-com, *The Unbalanced Equation*, is set for a September 2022 release. I needed a palate cleanser from fantasy so decided that an enemies-to-lovers rom-com about two geneticists living in Glasgow (I have a PhD in Molecular Genetics and have lived in Glasgow for 12 years now) was the perfect solution to this. I've had tonnes of fun writing it so I hope you'll consider reading it… even if it has no monsters!

Wow, there's certainly plenty for us to look forward to! Thank you for joining us!

Short Fiction

Glorious Monsters

D.N. Bryn

The masquerade charity ball was, above all else, filled with monsters.

Shane watched from the entrance to the spectacular ballroom as wealthy, masked investors in witch hats and werewolf tufts, demon horns and vampire fangs, all laughed and gossiped. Their skirts and capes swayed above the polished marble floor and their jewelry gleamed beneath the low chandeliers. Manicured nails clicked against glasses of deep red wine and bubbling champagne. Waiters in simple black outfits with white masks slipped through the fanciful crowd, offering appetizers topped in curls of edible gold. At the back of the room, a sweeping staircase wound up to balconies with scarlet carpeting where a few guests had already broken off to sit in relative seclusion.

They were the most glorious monsters Shane had ever witnessed.

Every costume had a human beneath it, of course – no business as upstanding as world-renowned Vitalis-Barron Pharmaceutical would be caught dead inviting rogue non-humans to their charity galas. But the monstrous masks and fancifully devilish disguises intrigued Shane. What was it about humans that made dressing as a monster, hiding beneath the mask of the enemy for an evening of frivolity, appeal so much to them?

Perhaps humanity just desperately wanted one day a year when they could look like something more vile than themselves and laugh about it.

That sounded like exactly the kind of premise Shane's editor would chew him out for presenting. His article on the Vitalis-Barron charity ball would be a fluff piece, she'd instructed, in terms clear as crystal – if that crystal had been cut into shards and gouged directly into his skull. But that was fine. Shane could survive one more fluff piece.

He hoped.

With a final adjustment to the white-feathered mask that covered his eyes, he set off into the crowd. He'd paired the mask with his nicest white button-up and black dress pants, and his neighbor had loaned him a lacy white shawl that gave the vague impression of a pair of folded wings. It created an ensemble far simpler than the rest of the crowd, but that minimalism made it easier for him to weave through the room, camera in hand, as he hunted down the most elaborately dressed attendees.

"You look amazing, what is your costume based on?" was his lead-in, followed by a few fluff-piece-worthy questions that he found various shades of dull, and finally, "I'm with ChatterDash Celebrity; do you mind if I snap a photo of you for an upcoming article?"

Shane had just finished with a woman dressed in fuzzy ears, a jewel-laden fur cloak, and seemingly nothing else when he turned directly into the shoulder of a tall man. The stranger's arm shot out, catching Shane's as he stumbled. Shane stammered an apology, wondering just how badly his light skin was flushing. One look at the man, and if he hadn't been turning pink before, he certainly would be now.

The stranger wore a vampire-themed costume, but compared to the elaborate frills and flourishes of other guests who'd chosen to go as the same monster, he'd taken a more understated approach: a black suit with a half-cape that gleamed a deep red on the inside, a small bejeweled pendant fastening it at his neck. His dark hair was slicked back behind his elaborate mask of blood-red twists. When he smiled at Shane, his fangs looked practically real.

"Aren't you delicious?" he said, his voice low and a little haunting

The blatant flirtation sparked an exhilarated flutter in Shane's stomach before he realized the man was likely playing into his costume; a pretend vampire sweet-talking a pretend snack.

"Cygnus, is it?" the stranger asked, nudging the largest of the white feathers dangling over the top of Shane's mask.

Cygnus. It took Shane a moment to place the name. "From the Greek myth? I suppose I must be."

"You're certainly lovely enough to be placed among the stars." The man smiled, and his dark eyes seemed to travel over Shane.

Was he genuinely flirting, then? If they were at Shane's favorite gay bar, he'd be absolutely certain. Here it was harder to know, surrounded by people he betted were primarily straight, and likely few to none of them trans like himself. But the way this man looked at him, Shane felt *known*, as though the stranger saw through every mask Shane wore, including the ones that didn't sit on his nose.

As Shane gawked, though, the stranger tipped his head with a soft, "I'll be seeing you, Cygnus."

He was gone before Shane could ask him a single one of the standard interview questions, much less for a picture. Which was a shame, because now that the man had vanished into the glittering crowd Shane really *wanted* that picture. Not for personal reasons, of course. Just for the article.

Shane did his best to latch onto a new target, but his heart felt even less in it than before. "I love the hat! You're a witch, then?"

"Yes, isn't the little black netting just so delightful? It's by Lemont Pierre." The woman extended a hand covered in lace and frills and what had to be a pound of diamond jewelry. "I'm Margaret Lane, by the way."

Shane was fairly certain she was one of Vitalis-Barron's high-level executives, but he'd prepped for this event just enough to scrape together his makeshift costume and no more. He shook her hand like it was the greatest honor, though, hoping that would suffice. "I'm Cygnus, apparently."

She stared at him blankly.

He flicked at the same feather the mysterious flirting stranger had. "The swan constellation?"

"Yes, right." Margaret Lane waved a hand. "I'm not much for astronomy, myself. Swan Lake, however, I do adore. You haven't *experienced* the ballet until you've seen the French tour from a box in the Jemison."

Shane could parse her statement just enough to know they were getting sorely off-topic, and he didn't want to be off-topic with any of these people. Except perhaps one man, who'd already run off anyway.

"I can imagine." He smiled so fakely it hurt and forged ahead. "Why did you choose to come as a witch tonight instead of, say, someone from a ballet?"

Fake or not, it was enough to entice a veritable essay out of the woman, including that she both didn't believe witches were real and was simultaneously afraid her niece was becoming one. The implications of this sparked Shane's interest more than most of the other prattle, but when she descended into conspiracy territory he cut her off long enough to snap her picture and disengage. He recorded the most useful – if not terribly interesting – tidbits in his notes, doing his best to avoid drooling over the chocolate cake the waiters were now serving. The chandeliers dimmed alongside an announcement that the floor was opening for a waltz.

A short lesson started up. Shane was clearly not wedged far enough out of the way because two women asked him to dance in quick succession, both of whom he gently turned down. He was just about to sneak up to the balconies to snap a few pictures of the dancing from above, when a familiar stranger slipped around him, the dark red underside of his cape shimmering as it flared and fell.

He extended his hand to Shane, dipping into a slight bow. His lips pulled back just enough to flash the tips of his costume fangs. “May I? That is, if you’re not already taken.”

Shane’s heartbeat quickened, but only partially from the nice kind of nerves; the other part told him to check over his shoulder for glares. This was not a gay bar, or a Pride festival, or any other kind of safe space for two men to dance. But the lights were still fairly low and everyone was masked. If a masquerade of anonymity and glamour wasn’t the time to let another man woo him on the dance floor, then what was?

He slipped the tips of his fingers into the mysterious stranger’s grasp, and Shane gave the man his first real smile of the evening. “I’d be honored.”

The stranger drew his thumb along the backs of Shane’s fingers and pulled him onto the ballroom dance floor. Around them, couples waltzed with varying levels of expertise. A few looked as though they’d given up on the real steps entirely and were simply swaying to the music, but the stranger drew Shane into the dance with the ease of considerable practice. He closed his fingers firmly around Shane’s and guided Shane’s other hand to his shoulder, pulling him a little closer as he cupped the middle of his back.

They set off. Shane felt himself fall perfectly into step, as though the stranger’s body was tied to his own by red ribbons, luring him back and forth in perfect rhythm. Each motion seemed to tighten their world down to just them and the music, the crowd turning to a blur of glitter and laughter.

One side of the stranger’s lips crooked higher than the other in a way that might have been a smirk or might have just been a natural part of him. "So, Cygnus, are you enjoying the ball?"

"It's certainly beautiful," Shane replied, his gaze never leaving the man in front of him. "Though what here could ever hold a candle to the night sky?" He gathered his courage enough to lift his hand, and his fingers came so close to the man's neck – to his fine jawline and his smirking mouth – that it felt like a thrill. He gently tapped the pendant holding the stranger's cloak in place. "Are you another Dracula, then? It's a common costume tonight."

"Perhaps I am," the stranger replied. "Or perhaps I'm merely your Phaethon."

"Doesn't Phaethon's overconfidence kill him in the end?" Shane was pretty sure that Cygnus had painstakingly collected his lover's bones for burial afterward.

"We all die eventually, but only the rare few are emblazoned in the stars." The all-too-beautiful stranger's eyes sparkled. "You're working on a piece for ChatterDash? Let me guess: seven best costumes of the rich and famous?"

"And one you won't believe!" Shane gave the mock tagline with a snort. He shook his head, almost losing his timing before the stranger pulled him back into tempo. "I don't judge anyone for wanting to fawn over pictures of gorgeous outfits – some days I want that, too. But there's so much more that could, and should, be said about a gala like this, about each choice that leads to a multi-million-dollar party of the rich and glamorous in the name of charity. And I wish that I could, occasionally, be paid to say those things."

"You're right." The stranger looked different for a moment, the swagger and the smirk gone – like someone almost human; almost ordinary. But his flirtatious demeanor returned as quickly as his grin. "Though I have to say, I would be very happy with an article that was simply pictures of one particular costume, worn by one particular Cygnus."

The feeling of butterflies tickled between Shane's ribs as he was swung out into a spin. The man pulled him back closer than before, arm wrapped tighter around his back. His hand crept up Shane's shoulder blades, and Shane's breath seemed to leave him for a moment as gentle fingers brushed Shane's neck, leaving nerves tingling in their wake.

"Swans have such exquisite necks, did you know that?" the man murmured, a shine running down his vampire fangs in the low chandelier light.

Shane's gaze caught on them; this was certainly flirtatious, but also an act in line with the costume. And, if Shane was being honest, it was a little bit delightful. "You're rather into this role play, aren't you?"

The stranger's voice went dark. "Who said I was playing a role?" A chill washed over Shane, broken a moment later by the man's laugh, the teasing tone so warm and joyous that Shane felt instantly relaxed. "I'm enjoying the freedom of the anonymity – that's one of your little interview questions, isn't it? Please, tell me your thoughts on that."

So near to the stranger, Shane felt light and a little dizzy. His gaze kept drifting to the man's lips.

"Anonymity?" he managed to say.

"Yes."

Shane swallowed, pulling his thoughts back into line. He could do this, even with a dangerously seductive man inches away. "Anonymity frees us all, as you said. For some, that means the freedom to flirt or dance with another man in a room of people who might judge. It's the freedom to be oneself by putting on the mask of another."

"And if the mask is yourself?" the stranger mused. "There's a kind of anonymity that comes from that, isn't there? When the mask is the self, then the wearer can pretend the person behind the mask *isn't*. For those whose actions are ordinarily judged, the mask provides safety, because all actions are seen as just an *act* and not a part of themselves."

"Safety," Shane repeated, thoughtful.

"Take vampires, for example. Where else could someone – vampire or not – comment on the beauty of a neck and have it seen as a valid form of flirtation and not a threat? But if the commenter is clear they're merely *pretending* to be a vampire, then suddenly…" He smirked again, and Shane could feel the man's gaze sweeping from his chin down to his collarbone. His tone turned somber, though, as his eyes lifted back to Shane's. "But perhaps it's even more than that. Did you know that vampires across the city have been leaving spontaneously – or one might say, vanishing? It's no wonder those remaining might wish to wear masks."

"Vampires have always come and gone more often than humans."

"Why is that?"

"I imagine they catch the attention of the police, and it forces them onward. For their safety." Shane hummed. "Their anonymity is lost, and with it their freedom."

"Indeed." The stranger continued to smile, but that expression seemed suddenly like a mask all of its own.

The song faded out then, and the man swept them toward the edge of the dance floor. He released Shane's hand and stepped back. The announcement of a break covered out whatever he said next, his voice bleeding into the sound of the speakers as his lips moved. With a bow, he turned back into the crowd.

Shane stood, staring after him.

The room seemed to lose a bit of its warmth and excitement with his departure.

Shane forced himself back to his work, but now his head wasn't in it. When the witch – Margaret Lane – badgered her way back into his attentions, he couldn't seem to do more than nod and smile. By the time he'd untangled himself, he traveled through the room at a brisk pace. He wasn't entirely sure what he was looking for at first, but the more turns he did off the floor, the more his gaze caught on anyone in a vampire costume. None of them were his mysterious stranger; that particular vampire seemed to have vanished as suddenly as those throughout the city. His heart sank.

He headed up the stairway to the balconies for one final attempt at finding him – for what, Shane didn't know. Was he going to ask the man for his number? This was likely only as exhilarating as it was because it *couldn't* go anywhere. But still, Shane wanted one last taste.

And after all the stranger had said, a creeping suspicion was growing in Shane's mind, one he didn't want to leave without uncovering the truth about.

Standing on the far curve of the balcony, he still saw no sign of the stranger. He should give up. Finish his job and go home. Or just go home; he had enough for the article, and the lights were dimmed too far now to take proper pictures of individual costumes. He stood at the railing to snap a few final shots of the chandeliers and the people swirling beneath, but as he turned to go, his chest caught.

The stranger leaned against the column that provided semi-privacy for the couches along the wall, a half-empty wine glass dangling from one hand. He held out a plate with the other. It held a slice of the mouth-watering dark chocolate cake that had been served before the dance. "I thought to bring you a drink, but this was what your gaze kept stealing back to. Well, the cake and me."

"What can I say – I have an eye for fine delicacies?" It sounded more like an awkward question than any natural form of flirting, but it brought a sincere laugh from the stranger, so the embarrassment felt worth it. Shane accepted the cake gingerly, leaning against the column beside the man. He took a small bite – it was just as delicious as it looked – before venturing, "Would you mind terribly if I took a picture of your costume?"

"You still think this is a costume?"

"I think it could be more than that," Shane replied, "Or you could just as easily be teasing me with all this talk of vampires in masks."

As he pushed his fork back into the cake, the stranger caught his wrist. Shane flinched, but the man's grip didn't falter. He lifted Shane's hand toward his mouth, pressing against the tendons to force Shane's fingers to extend, and pricked the pad of one on his fang.

The sensation was sharp and pleasurable, like a shot of fine liquor. For a moment Shane wanted to leave his finger there and let the man's lips close around it. Then reality caught up with him. He pulled away.

The stranger let him go. "Is that real enough for you?"

Shane tucked his pricked finger against his palm. He was breathing a little harder, from exhilaration but also from fear. They were up here in the dark, and this man – this vampire – had proven himself to be quite forward. Aggressively forward, even. Or did Shane only now see things that way because he *was* a vampire? Because it wasn't all an act?

What had seemed a grand adventure while it was an anonymous game was far more dangerous with the masks off.

"I could call for security, you know," Shane whispered.

"I'd prefer it if you didn't." The vampiric stranger's voice was soft, but it lacked the darkness he'd employed earlier. He smiled and took a sip from his wine, his attention wandering to the crowd below. "Eat your cake, Cygnus."

Shane licked a bit of chocolate frosting off his fork and stared at the vampire. "You're not planning to eat *me*, are you?"

"I admit that would be very nice, if you were offering." But his gaze barely flickered over Shane's neck before he fixed on Shane's eyes. "Do you think me a monster?"

"Aren't you?" Shane taunted. "Cornering swans in the dark."

The vampire's lips twitched. "Far be it from me not to play a bit heavy on the stereotypes when I have such an opportunity as this. Besides, you haven't exactly protested."

"I didn't exactly know what I was getting into."

"But you do now. And you're still here."

Shane *was* still there, even with his escape to the stairs unblocked and a pair of discreet security guards within earshot. He found he didn't want to *be* anywhere else. Despite his lingering worries, knowing the stranger was a vampire had only made him more enticing. But it also raised the question of why he had come to this gala of wealthy humans at all, sneaking into a place he had surely not been invited to, full of people who wore his visage as a costume but who would turn on him the moment they knew what he was. "What you said about certain people wearing the mask of themselves to act as who they are in safety: is that why you're here – to be yourself?"

"It's a perk, like meeting you. But no." The vampire gave the slightest bow, flourishing the edge of his short cape. "I'm here to commit a crime." He glanced past Shane to the stairwell, where Margaret Lane the faux-witch was ascending, one hand lifting her ornately embroidered skirt. His lips lifted, revealing the full extent of his fangs. "And there's the crime coming right up."

He drew off his cape in a smooth motion, laying it inside out over his arm like a draped towel of shimmering red. Switching out his ornate mask for a simple white server's guise so quickly that Shane only caught a glimpse of cheekbones, he scooped up a serving tray from the floor. With the return of his darkly dashing smile he lifted his half-full wine glass toward Shane.

"To Cygnus," he said. "May he never need mourn this lover in this life." Shane watched him go, his heart pounding in his chest.

He was here to commit a crime, he'd said, which implied he should be stopped. Yet Shane could do nothing but watch as the vampire sauntered to the stairs, colliding with Margaret as she reached the top. His wine toppled, spilling down the front of her shirt.

The woman's earlier harmless self-importance transformed into something beastly as she berated him. Shane was taken aback by the humility the vampire returned, looking in that moment so much smaller and less dangerous than he had all that evening. But perhaps that too was a mask he wore often.

He consoled Margaret by offering to show her past the roped off hallway that led away from the balconies to the private upstairs restroom. Shane edged after them, right up to the velvet rope, just in time to watch the vampire grab Margaret and pull her out of view.

His stomach knotted, and he glanced toward the security guards. He could still shout for them, disrupt the vampire's scheme before it could harm Margaret. But Shane wanted to know what the vampire was up to more than he cared to save Margaret Lane just yet. Perhaps the man under his swan costume was a little bit of a monster himself tonight.

Shane snuck past the rope and down the hall. He could hear voices in a distant, muffled way, but he couldn't tell which of the three doors they were coming from. As he moved past the last one, the sounds grew crisper, slipping in from the open veranda that overlooked the twinkling gardens where a few guests still meandered. Shane sprinted out the door, following the voices to their origin: the cracked windows of a room along the veranda's edge.

The inside was still dark, the curtains hanging loose, but he could just make out their silhouettes through the glass door. The vampire had pinned Margaret Lane stiffly against the wall, his fangs bared. Her witch's hat lay at their feet.

"You are the monsters," he growled, "wearing our faces in your ghoulish party while your company feasts on our flesh."

"I don't know what you're talking about," Margaret snapped.

"Are you so sure about that?" The vampire leaned closer, leering over her. "Tell me the truth, now: your people *are* the reason so many vampires have gone missing."

The knot in Shane's stomach tightened further. Perhaps the vampiric stranger wasn't the only one committing crimes here.

Margaret, to her credit, didn't shrink beneath him, but her voice sounded increasingly less steady. "Why should I tell you anything?"

The vampire let the question linger, his lips sinking toward her ear. Shane could just barely hear him as he spoke, dark and soft. "I can feel your fear."

With a little shriek, Margaret tried to jerk away from him, but he held her against the wall again as though her protests were barely a nuance. "Have you ever been bitten before, Miss Lane? There's an intoxicant in our fangs, like a drug to keep the human quiet and happy, but I can choose whether to employ it or not. For you, I can make the pain rather substantial indeed." His words twisted with a bitter humor. "Though with how much you hate my kind, perhaps it'll hurt you more to be bitten and to *like* it."

The three of them – the vampire, Margaret, and Shane still watching transfixed from the external balcony – all startled as a knock sounded at the door. "Margaret, is that you? They want to make the final toast."

Margaret screamed, yanking against the vampire's grip. The person outside cursed and rattled the door, but its lock held. Shane stood in rapt silence as they shouted for security, their calls fading as they ran back toward the ballroom.

The vampire hissed. "These days if a vampire goes

around biting people at their leisure – even happily consenting people – they're likely to disappear, and buying blood on the black market is more expensive than ever. I hear some vampires are avoiding all that by keeping a snack in their basement." He must have tightened his grip because Margaret yelped in pain. "You make us vanish, we make you vanish."

A little sob came out of Margaret, but it couldn't mask her disgust and bitterness. "If you lay so much as a fang on me, my people will hunt you down like the monster you are."

He bared his teeth. "Like you've done to those other vampires?"

"Yes, fine, that's what you want to hear, isn't it?" She cackled, the sound more stereotypically witchy than any costume. "But what can you possibly do about it? You could take vengeance on me, but this city would only hate your kind all the more. We're doing them a favor by eliminating you. If they realized it, they would thank us."

So it was true. The admission made Shane feel hollow. This had been going on and no one had noticed, no one had cared. Because vampires were monsters, weren't they? Monsters to be worn as costumes by the very humans who forced them to seek the safety of masks in the first place.

The vampire reacted to this news with another hiss, but his posture shifted. "They probably would." He sounded sad, and as though he wasn't truly talking to Margaret anymore.

When he sank his teeth into her neck it seemed in

resignation instead of aggression. His whole body heaved like a sob while he drank. Shane watched in horror, not sure who the feeling was for – the vampire for doing this, himself for letting this happen, or Margaret for deserving it. She went limp. The vampire dropped her. Shane swallowed down something acidic in the back of his throat, but when Margaret moaned from the floor, he let himself exhale. She was alive.

All that she'd done to vampires, and the stranger hadn't even killed her.

A clatter rose down the hall on the interior side of the room, turning quickly to banging as a woman shouted, "Security! Open up!"

The vampire slid his cape back on and turned toward the glass veranda door – toward Shane.

Shane wrapped both hands around the doorknob. He was certain he was no match for the vampire in strength, but if he chose to, he could hold it in place long enough for security to make it around to this side of the building, with their tasers and guns ready to take the vampire down. To make him vanish, like others of his kind.

"Ah, we meet again, my swan." The vampire came to a stop just on the other side of the glass. His mask was crooked now, his smile beneath even more so. "Is this where Phaethon dies?"

He didn't move as the pounding continued and Margaret stirred, hoarsely calling for help. He didn't force the door open. He simply watched Shane, looking soft in the moonlight as it shone through the glass, cutting deep shadows along his mask.

Shane opened the door and tipped his head toward the gardens. "Go."

It didn't feel like enough, and as the vampire slipped by him, lunging for the veranda railing, he wished he could add something else: *Be safe. Live free. I'm not a swan, and you're not a god, and neither of us should have to die to be remembered.*

But then the vampire turned back and lunged at Shane.

Shane didn't flinch, and in the last moment, the vampire came to a stop with one hand resting so lightly against Shane's cheek that it seemed little more than a breeze. His lips pressed gently to Shane's, soft and haunting. Then he drew back. He smiled again, one fang-tip still visible.

As he leaped into the garden, cape flaring behind him, Shane smiled back.

The security team rounded the far edge of the veranda an instant later with shouts of "There! Down below!" as Margaret howled about a vampire assailant.

But Shane just tucked himself out of the way – a simple swan in a simple mask – and watched the vampire disappear across the grounds, thinking of all the articles he would never write about this night. He had come looking for monsters, and he had certainly found them. Glorious monsters, indeed. Shane pressed his fingers to his lips.

A single glorious monster, at least.

D.N. Bryn is an author of speculative fiction and queer fantasy romance. The characters in this short story will return in Bryn's upcoming series of vampire romances, starting fall 2022! Until then, you can find their other universe of reimagined mythological species in a 1930s steampunk-inspired setting in the These Treacherous Tides series.

Lead Me Not Into Temptation

Josie Jaffrey

<u>CONTENT WARNING</u>

This story contains references to suicide and postpartum psychosis.

Arthur was the first to arrive at the college suite. It was just as he had always imagined it: wood-panelled, wood-floored, ragged-armchaired and saturated with the cigarette smoke of countless students who had come before him. The two bedrooms were of similar proportions, each with a narrow bed, desk and sink, so similar that there was little to choose between them, yet still he did not claim one. It seemed impolite to do so before he had met the fellow with whom he would be sharing the space. Instead, he pulled out his Latin primer and started brushing up on his grammar in preparation for the first week of term.

George was late. George was always late, although Arthur didn't know this yet. When the suite's door crashed open a couple of hours later, it was clear that he was also more than a little drunk.

"Hello there, chap," George slurred. His collar was askew and it looked as though he had been wearing his clothing since the previous night. It was both too formal and too dishevelled for this time of the morning. "You'd be the fellow I'm bunking with, would you?"

Arthur had already risen to his feet and now stretched out his hand towards his inebriated fellow student. "Arthur Morris," he said. "Studying Greats."

"George Cholmondley, mostly studying rugger and rowing, I hope." George clasped Arthur's hand tightly in his own large, sticky one, shook it once, then dropped without ceremony into one of the armchairs and fell instantly asleep.

It was an inauspicious beginning, indeed, but what can you tell from the beginning of anything?

George and Arthur went everywhere together or, more accurately, George was good-natured enough to invite Arthur everywhere he went and Arthur was grateful to be included. In that way, slowly, they became a common sight together around the quad, Arthur dragging George to tutorials and George dragging Arthur to the pub. George had become the college's top rower by the end of his first term, thanks mostly to Arthur's diligence in rousing him from bed early enough to get on the water for practice each morning, and Arthur had become something of a social butterfly by following George's example. All in all, the two could not have been better paired.

Until Lily.

Daughter of the college chaplain, Lily had been

granted early admission to the university on the proviso that she continue to live with her parents in their college lodgings. This was not only convenient for her classes, but also put her in the unusual position of being one of the very few eligible young women with whom the hundreds of male students had regular contact. It was inevitable that flirtations and infatuations would occur. For some young ladies, that prospect might have intimidated. As it happened, Lily was more than fit for the challenge.

Unsurprisingly, the first encounter between the three was incited by George. It was a Saturday rugby match, the last of the term. George was on the pitch, Arthur was on the bench with his belongings and Lily was in the front row of the stands, cheering along with the crowd.

Perhaps, since her allure has thus far been described only so far as it pertains to her value as a novelty in the male-dominated world of academia, you might imagine Lily to be quite plain. You would be quite wrong. She was not beautiful, not exactly, but she was magnetic. She was bright-eyed and full-lipped, but it was the brashness of her laughter and the way she surrendered to it fully, her head tipped back with abandon, that drew Arthur's attention. Even after months under George's tutelage, he still couldn't imagine feeling settled enough in his skin that he could yield so entirely to emotion.

Arthur couldn't stop watching her. He tried to concentrate on the game, but he soon lost track of play. Eventually, he turned away from the pitch and gave himself over to the study of her face, which meant he was watching when she saw George. The ball had rolled to a stop on the grass just in front of her seat. George was the one sent to collect it and bring it back to the field, but he only accomplished the first of those tasks. Even from a distance, Arthur could see Lily's pupils dilate. When he followed her gaze, it was with resignation that he recognised his friend as the source of her bedazzlement.

She stooped to pick up the ball for him, passing it from her hands to his with an intensity forged in fluttered lashes and parted lips. Their fingers touched in the exchange, George's movements leisurely and deliberate as a smile spread across his face. And what a smile.

Arthur couldn't blame Lily for her reaction; he had to admit that George was worth staring at. In his rugby kit, mud-smeared and bare-thighed, he drew the eye. You would never have known that he'd woken up that morning in the bath, reeking of stale cognac and still wearing his suit from the night before, as usual. With his dark hair and pink cheeks, he was almost as vivid as Lily herself. Seeing them together, they looked as though they belonged to each other.

From that point on, the college considered their fates sealed. George, ever the gentleman, introduced Lily to Arthur that same day and took pains to include him in every outing the undeclared couple enjoyed together. This was uncomfortable for everyone except, apparently, for George himself.

And so it was with relief that George's two satellites saw him reclaimed by his raucous family for the Christmas break. They would both stay at college, Lily with her family in the chaplain's lodgings and Arthur in the echoing loneliness of the rooms he shared with George, with no expectation that he should meet the girl again until his return.

It was grey and rainy the day everything changed: Boxing Day, the disappointing chaser to what had been a far from white Christmas. Lily was finishing her lunch alone in the refectory, seeking a brief respite from her family under the guise of visiting the library. She didn't expect to see anyone she knew.

"Merry Christmas." Arthur took the seat across from hers.

"Oh." She arranged her cutlery on her empty plate and neatly dabbed at the corners of her mouth. "I thought you would be going home for Christmas."

Arthur smiled ruefully. He looked tired, as though the break from his studies were doing him more harm than good. Perhaps, if he had nowhere to go, that was precisely the case.

"You don't have family to visit?" she asked.

"I'm an orphan. There's no one eager for my company at this time of year."

"That's awful."

Arthur's face fell.

"I'm sorry," Lily continued. "I didn't mean to be insensitive. I only meant…" She wasn't sure what she had meant, but she knew she couldn't leave things as they were, with her cheeks heating and the young man opposite her looking increasingly wretched.

"Please," he said, forcing a smile. "There's no need to feel uncomfortable. I'm perfectly happy with my lot in life. I've been very fortunate, truly, to be admitted here on scholarship. This is my home now."

His hopeful words broke Lily's heart. Here she was, trying to escape her family, when Arthur had no family left from whom to escape. George was all he had, and she had even tried to deny him that. She had behaved shabbily, and it was time she made amends.

"Come for dinner with my family," she said.

"Oh, no." Arthur looked down at his hands. "Please, there's no need to extend your pity to me. I have no desire to impose."

"You won't be imposing. And I'd like you to come. Please. It would make me happy."

To her surprise, Lily found that the words she'd spoken were true. Arthur must have heard that in her voice, because he agreed to the invitation and thus embarked on an evening so wonderful, so revelatory, that he wondered how he and Lily had ever been less than friends. They laughed as they ate, as they played party games with her family, as they relaxed by the fire late into the evening, long after the rest of the family had retired to their beds.

Lily was entranced. How could it be that she had never truly seen this boy before, with his gentle face, his soft voice, and the way he snatched glances at her, as though he were rationing them against future need? Subtly, smile by smile, glance by glance, she found herself overcome by his quiet charm.

The only sour note that evening was the behaviour

of her father. Usually a genial and welcoming man, Lily was surprised to find that he had taken against Arthur.

The truth was that, since the moment he had invited the young man inside his home, the chaplain had felt increasingly uneasy. There was a chill rushing up and down his neck, yet the doors and windows were firmly closed and no one else complained of a draught. His fingertips felt as though they were frozen, no matter how close he held them to the fire, and the trembling in his hands was so pronounced as he tried to cut the ham for dinner that he had to cede the carving duties to Arthur. And all the time, throughout the evening, he felt as though there were eyes fixed on him, eyes with evil intent, even when there was no one looking in his direction at all. It made the chaplain unsure and defensive, which manifested in ill humour towards their guest – whose proximity, strangely enough, seemed only to exacerbate the chaplain's condition.

The moment Arthur left, the man's body was at peace.

But from that night on, his heart and soul could find no rest.

By the time George returned to college, laden with gifts and cheer, any awkwardness between Lily and Arthur had disappeared entirely. George, the merry naif, thought that the newfound accord between his friend and potential lover could only be a good thing. He saw nothing in it but the increase of their group's happiness for the future. Little did he know how short that future would be.

Over the course of the following term, the three became as close as it was proper for two men and an unmarried woman to be. Closer, perhaps.

Lily was not unaccustomed to male attention. She didn't court it, not openly, because the game lay in drawing the men to her. Besides, it was necessary to make some pretence of modesty and decorum, if only for the sake of her father's reputation. He had been behaving so oddly since Christmas, insisting she stay away from the male students, that it seemed wise to humour him. Her restraint lasted only so long, though. The moment she was away from prying eyes, she could conduct herself however she wished.

And she fully intended so to do.

With George and Arthur, the game had been long. She teased and baited, all the while appearing nothing less than chaste as she laughed her raucous laugh, and yet neither of them bit. The problem was, she believed, that they were each too loyal to the other to break the trust between them. If just one of them could have her, thus depriving the other, then neither of them would.

To Lily, this was a matter of no small frustration. But she was willing to work to find a solution, and it so happened that the perfect occasion for mischief was soon upon them.

There was much spoken of the college's masquerade ball. It was an annual tradition that, at the end of Lent, the students and faculty would mask their faces and mingle amongst each other in liquor-drenched freedom. Designed to create a freer atmosphere for the exchange of scholarly ideas, in fact the event was best known as something of a debauch, allowing lines to be crossed in anonymity that might otherwise have remained unbreached. So it proved for Arthur and Lily, for – much to her own surprise – it was Arthur on whom she had primarily fixed her sights.

He was not a handsome man, not athletic or strong of jaw like George, but he could be beautiful. Lily had seen that, finally, over the Christmas break, and now she could see nothing else. He had grace and poise, deftness and delicacy of speech and movement, and something else besides, something Lily couldn't put into words, but that felt almost ethereal. However unable she was to describe how Arthur's proximity made her feel, she knew that she wanted it again. She'd live in it if she could, if she could but dare it, if she could avoid George, and if she could only convince Arthur to accept it.

By mutual agreement, all three friends arrived at the masquerade alone, in costumes they had not revealed to each other beforehand. It was part of the fun, Lily had told George, but secretly she had hoped she might identify Arthur before he did and spirit him away. It was uncharitable to desert George, perhaps, but with Lily due to spend the Easter break away with her family, it was the only opportunity she would have to be alone with Arthur before the summer.

It was now or never.

Arthur wasn't sure about his costume. George had told him this was an opportunity to break free from themselves, to surprise their peers with masks that were the exact opposite of who they really were. If that was the intent, then George had missed the mark with the costume he had selected for Arthur: a black Venetian mask with devil horns and a suit with tails to match. If George thought him the opposite of a devil, Arthur feared he was much mistaken. With the thoughts that were crowding his head this evening, he felt far from angelic.

He knew Lily the moment she walked into the quad. Whatever she'd worn, he would have known the defiant tip of her head, the determined set of her jaw, and the elegant shape of her long neck. Even without the lily she had tucked behind her ear for his benefit, he would have recognised her just as quickly.

They slipped away alone before Lily had even greeted George. It was a betrayal, Arthur knew, but it was also the culmination of everything George had taught him over the past six months. He couldn't turn Lily down, not now he knew what it meant when her eyes softened as she looked at him. This was something he simply had to do.

They passed through a wooded courtyard arbored with roses, blooming out of season, and it was there that Lily entwined her fingers with Arthur's and led him beneath the trees. There he let her put his back against the bark and press her lips to his neck, to his cheek, to his lips. It was cold enough that their breath was visible between their faces, and yet still they delayed in the permissive dark and claimed each other's mouths, hers demanding and his shy.

As their kisses became more urgent, Lily became

aware of the limitations of their trysting spot. It was not enough to kiss him, to touch his cheek, to feel his body pressed against hers. She needed more, and this was not the appropriate venue.

There was only one place to go.

Taking his hand in hers, she led him across the college. He had to smuggle her up the staircase to the rooms he shared with George, ducking around corners as he listened carefully for the footsteps of their fellow students. Once they were safely in the suite, shut away in his room with two doors between them and the outside world, such caution was quickly abandoned. Things moved so fast from that point that it spun Lily's head, and later she couldn't imagine what had come over her to inspire such desperate hunger for the man in her arms. She might almost have believed she'd imagined it, if there had not been a witness. The worst possible witness. George.

He was standing in the doorway to Arthur's room, left unlocked in their haste, his mouth open, face white. Perhaps he had seen them slip away from the quad. Perhaps he had come back to the suite for some forgotten item. Perhaps he had simply had enough of the ball without the two of them present. Either way, he had chosen the worst possible moment to appear.

Arthur was propped up on his hands with Lily's legs wrapped around his waist. Both were naked. There was no disguising their predicament.

Arthur's face fell as his eyes met his friend's.

"George." He looked as though he wanted to say more, but the words didn't come. For several long seconds they were stuck in that painful tableau, nothing but silence and despair between the three of them, until George turned abruptly and left the room.

The night ended quickly after that. Lily's exit from the suite was swift and silent and, she vowed, never to be repeated. She hadn't realised that George truly cared for her, not as anything more than a friend, but the look on his face…

That look.

It was as though his heart were breaking in two.

As she was to discover, his was not the only one.

Arthur's costume was found folded neatly on the bridge the next morning, the devil's mask balanced on top and his shoes placed underneath the pile, a sock stuffed inside each one, as though he had been hoping to keep his outfit clean and dry for his return. But there would be no return for Arthur. Later that morning, the police found a smear of blood and hair on one of the bridge abutments beneath where his clothes had been piled. The water was high that day. If there had been any other trace of his descent, it was washed away with the rain.

Arthur left nothing else behind except the belongings in his room and the child that would soon begin to grow in Lily's womb.

The memorial service was more packed than anyone had expected it would be, so packed that there were rows of mourners standing at the back of the college chapel as Lily's father led the service. At first, Lily assumed they were all friends of George's, and George assumed they had come only for the scandal, but as they conversed with one after another in the quad afterwards, it became clear that Arthur had been far better known and better liked than either of them had appreciated. He had no family, but there were countless men who seemed to consider him a brother and enough women claimed him as a 'dear friend' to make a Lothario blush. It was strange how learning of Arthur's proximity to others, so out of character for the man they'd known, made him feel that much more out of reach to them. Who was this man, who had been their friend? They were no longer sure, but far from tarnishing him in their eyes, the unsolvable mystery of the man they'd both loved just made them yearn for him more.

Drawn together in their grief and guilt, George and Lily were swiftly married. Never much of a mathematician, George was unsure whether the baby growing within his new wife was his or Arthur's, but it was of no consequence: the couple were happy to raise the child together either way.

The chaplain was not happy, however. So unhappy was he, in fact, that he refused to perform the marriage ceremony for his daughter. Although he had no objection to George – the boy seemed fit enough, if a little addled by his knocks on the rugby pitch – he was disturbed by the changes that had started manifesting in his daughter after young Mr Morris's death; by suicide, the chaplain assumed. He'd been loath to give a memorial service for someone whose demise had taken such a sinful form, but after all there was no definitive proof, and Lily had insisted. It was the last thing upon which he had allowed her to insist.

There had been a dreadful row. It was clear that there was something wrong with his Lily, something working upon her, turning her from a dutiful, devoted daughter and student into a wild creature who would not be contained indoors, would not talk to her family, would not even attend church. Some of this might have been explained by her pregnancy, but Lily kept that information to herself. It was only after the marriage – performed in secret in Scotland – that the truth came to light. Yet even after she had obtained her husband, the chaplain saw no improvement in his daughter's mental state. In fact, it became steadily worse.

By the time he received news of the birth of his grandson, the chaplain had not spoken to his daughter for six months. He would never have a chance to do so again, for within a day of the birth announcement came news of Lily's death.

George was not made for solitude. Isolated from his family, left in a shabby townhouse with an infant son, his wet-nurse and nothing but the ghosts of his former confidantes for company, he felt that any day he might follow in Lily's footsteps and lose his own mind.

He hadn't told her family the truth of it, because it was enough that he had to bear it himself, but her death had not been a peaceful one. It had started towards the end of her pregnancy, as she felt the little life quickening inside her. The more he kicked, the more agitated she became, until finally she declared her intention to rid her body of the parasite it harboured.

The doctor had strapped her down then, but Lily only writhed and kicked in her restraints, yelling all sorts of crazy things: that she was carrying the child of the devil, that it was evil, that she'd been impregnated by an incubus, that the child would be a demon too, that it had to die or it would ruin them all…

When George could no longer stand her screams, the doctor kept her sedated until the birth. He had hoped it would be the turning point, but if anything her psychosis only intensified. She screamed when she finally saw the baby's face, shouting obscenities, denouncing him as the child of Satan. Fearing she might intend harm towards him, George sent for a wet-nurse and took the baby away.

Whatever evil Lily had seen, George could not discern it. He was enchanted by the tiny creature. There was no malice in its little pink face. He looked into its new eyes and saw only the innocence of every child, untarnished and desiring nothing but the care of a loving parent, which he swore he would provide just as dutifully as any mother. He began as he meant to continue, cradling the little boy for every waking second that he was not being fed, lavishing his attention on him to the exclusion of all others. Given Lily's incapacitation, he felt that he owed nothing less to his son, but the new father's devotion to his baby was his mother's demise.

Lily had been sedated following the birth, but her restraints had not been reattached. While the household was distracted by the baby, she found her peace on the cobblestoned pavement five storeys beneath her bedroom window.

These were the truths George kept locked in his mind until it threatened to break beneath their weight. He tried to face it all with denial, naming his new son Arthur after the boy's potential father and his own erstwhile friend, but he was still haunted by the too-recent losses, hollowed out so deeply that even the sight of his son's smile could not fill him up again. He clung to it nonetheless, to every cry and snuffle and gurgle, but found the spectre of his old friend's face was too present on his son's own for him to forget what he had lost.

It was in this state, with the anniversary of Arthur Morris's death approaching, that he received an invitation to the college's masquerade ball. Whether by way of penance or tribute, he sent his acceptance by return of post.

The quad looked exactly the same, and yet entirely different. Candles that a year ago had streamed merrily in their lanterns now felt blindingly garish, the drinks were unpalatable and the masks, so exciting at his first masquerade, were now less mysterious than they were alienating. George, wearing the same jester's outfit he had donned a year ago, felt locked into a lifetime as the proverbial sad clown. He had chosen this costume both literally and by every small misstep that had brought him through the past twelve months. He felt each one like a pin in his heart.

Arthur and Lily, together.

Arthur, gone.

Then Lily.

Arthur.

The figure caught George's eye at the edge of the quad as it headed under an archway and through into the small garden beyond. At this time of year, there shouldn't be any roses blooming, and yet the arbors beyond the arch were heavy with blooms and their scent. The man stopped there beneath the trees, graceful and delicate, a man wearing a suit with tails and a black devil's mask.

It couldn't be.

Arthur was dead. Arthur died a year ago.

George's head knew this well enough, but his feet weren't listening. They guided him across the quad, pushing through groups of students and tutors gathered around the braziers, his eyes blind to everything except his destination. He knew from the moment he saw the mask, but until there was grass under his shoes and Arthur's eyes were reflected in his own, he did not truly believe.

"It's you," he whispered into the darkness.

The darkness whispered back. "It's me, George. I was hoping you would come."

As Arthur stepped out from beneath the trees, George could doubt it no longer. It was truly him, back from the dead, waiting for him at the masquerade as George had hoped he would be twelve months ago. If he allowed himself to fall into the moment, perhaps he might forget, for tonight at least, that the last year had happened at all. Tonight, perhaps this could be the truth instead.

"Are you really here?"

"Yes," Arthur said. "And no. But I am as good as here."

The words made no sense to George, but he couldn't find it in himself to care. All he cared about was that Arthur was here, in front of him, and that he could finally say all the things he had left unsaid for so long.

"I should have told you," George said, closing the distance between them. "I should have told you so many things."

"You didn't need to." Arthur reached out and pulled the mask from George's face, letting it fall to the ground, and cupped George's cheek in his lithe fingers. "I knew. And I'm sorry. I would have done things differently if the choice had been mine."

"And now?"

Arthur didn't answer, but George saw the eyes behind the mask flicker down to his mouth, and that was invitation enough. He leaned forward and kissed the lips he had loved so long, entwined his clumsy fingers in the hair at the back of Arthur's head, pressed his heart against the heart he had pined for and felt its steady beat.

Thud-thud.

It was a long time before George could compose himself enough to pull away. When he finally did, he saw sadness in Arthur's eyes.

"I have to go."

George could only nod numbly in reply, his hands falling from his lover's face, from his hair, as he tried fruitlessly to untwine his heart as well.

"The baby?" Arthur asked.

"A boy. I named him after you."

Something was happening, a blurring of Arthur's body, as though he were being caught up in a black sandstorm that had no substance, brought no breeze, but nonetheless began to erase the edges of his form. George snatched at him, trying to hold his love in place, but his fingers closed around thin air. Arthur's last words were distorted by the dark nothingness that was rising between them, but George heard them clearly enough.

"If you love me, keep our boy safe."

"I will," George whispered. "I do and I will. I promise."

It was a promise he never broke.

Eighteen years later, Arthur Junior took up his place at the college.

There were a lot of Arthurs that year, all following in their father's footsteps. The original Arthur was long gone, far away on the other side of the continent, sowing the seed of devilry in pastures new. It wouldn't be long before each one of his sons would do the same, however reluctantly.

Josie Jaffrey is an indie author of urban fantasy, paranormal romance and young adult fantasy who lives in Oxford, England. If you enjoyed this short story, you might enjoy May Day, the first book in Josie's Seekers series. It's an urban fantasy novel featuring a chaotic vampire detective with a serious grudge against the only man who can help her solve her latest case.

My Granny, The Dragon

Gemma Church

I stopped telling people that Granny was a dragon for three reasons. One: they always laughed at me. Two: they said I was mad. Three: one day, scales started appearing on my chest.

"They're not scales, that's eczema," Mum said when I showed her in the bath.

"Then why are they blue?" I asked.

But she just smiled as mums do when they're not really listening to you, handing me a towel.

When I showed them to Granny at the hospice, she was far more understanding. She put on her thick reading glasses and peered at my skinny chest.

"Interesting." She sat back in her armchair and exhaled a puff of smoke. "Your grandad had blue scales too."

I pulled down my t-shirt and sat opposite her on a footstool, opening the biscuit barrel that always sat next to her armchair. "What does that mean? Blue scales?"

"That's the best type, George! Blue dragons are the rarest kind and, I would argue, the best kind. They're the best flyers. The ones that'll fly higher than any other sort of dragon you'll find out there."

"What do red scales mean, then?"

"Why, they're red to match my red-hot temper and long red hair, of course!"

She pretended to roar, sticking up her clawed hands and exposing her dentures. I laughed, because I didn't have the heart to remind Granny that she was as bald as a football and had been for as long as I could remember.

She was always a bit stuck back in time, was Granny. Forgetting things from yesterday, but remembering old times as quick as a flash. Mum called it, "dementia". But Mum also called my dragon scales "eczema". So, what did she know?

Like most grannies, mine spoiled me rotten. I could eat as many biscuits as I wanted, she didn't nag me about my homework, and she answered all my questions without getting grumpy. But, unlike most grannies, she would also toast me marshmallows with her fiery breath and take me for long flights over the countryside near her house, doing great loop-the-loops, me with my arms around her neck as we soared into the sky.

When I was four, I assumed everyone's granny was a dragon, and so I didn't worry about it. But when I started school, I realised my granny wasn't like other grannies. Their grannies were all doughy-skinned and smelt of rotting flowers. My granny was covered in scales and smelt of Silk Cut cigarettes. Those scales cover her entire body and face now but started off as small patches, she once told me. "And I was quite beautiful back in the day but with every change, a little more of the dragon remains."

"What's wrong with your gran's skin?" said Mark, a boy in my year with as much tact as a house brick, when Granny picked me up from school one day. She was wearing her favourite yellow shawl, covering her head and most of her face. "Did they try to burn her as a witch back in the old days?"

I asked Granny about that, asking when she was distracted, washing the dishes, because I was too embarrassed to ask her face-to-face. She just laughed.

"A witch? What a silly boy! They haven't burnt witches since the Middle Ages, how old does he think I am? Besides, do witches have these?"

And she pushed out her wings then, tearing big holes in her cardigan and eclipsing the sun streaming through the kitchen window. She turned to face me, hands outstretched and still covered in suds. Her silhouette was like one of those statues that you see in church, looking down with true grace and beauty. But Granny's face wasn't all docile like some sappy saint. She had fire in her soul instead.

Every time I asked Granny about being a dragon, she always went quiet and said she would tell me when I was a bit older. But I'm not a very patient person, so I asked my mum about it once instead. My, how she yelled at me.

"How dare you call your granny a dragon! After all she's done for you and for this country. Don't you ever let me hear you saying that again!" And she smacked me so hard with her slippers that I couldn't sit down the next day in school without letting out a little yelp of pain.

I was too scared to ask Mum again, not wanting to point out that I didn't *call* Granny a dragon, I just wanted to know why Granny *was* a dragon. But I don't think my mum ever saw things the same way as I did.

One day when I popped into Granny's house, she was particularly quiet. She didn't fly. She didn't toast marshmallows. She didn't even make a brew. So I popped on the kettle instead and tottered into the front room with two mugs of steaming tea and a plate full of ginger biscuits balancing on a tray.

"George!" she cried, swooping over to me, and taking the tray from my hands. "What have I told you about using that kettle! I don't want you burning yourself."

"It's fine, Granny. I make tea all the time for Mum."

Granny gulped down the scorching hot tea as she always did, licking her cracked lips. "Your mother should know better than that. Letting you boil a kettle."

She tutted and then she went all quiet again, looking out the window, her scorched, scaly fingers worrying the net curtains. She pushed back her wig and gazed outside, as if forgetting I was there. She still wore a wig back then and pencilled in where her eyebrows should have been. And she always had a handkerchief up her cardigan sleeve to dab her nose, on account of her not having any nose hair either.

"Are you all right, Granny?"

It was probably the first time I'd thought to ask

Granny how she was. She was just one of those people who was a constant in my life, always old and always smiling. But today she looked ancient, and she wasn't smiling.

"I'll be fine," she said, signalling to the only photo of Grandad she had in the house. He was grinning and looking smart in his RAF uniform. "It would have been his birthday today, that's all. So I'm a bit lost in my memories."

I knew from Mum that her dad, my grandad, had died before she was born. He'd survived the war and then got himself killed in a motorcycle crash, wearing a helmet and obeying the 30 mile-an-hour speed limit.

Granny gazed at the photograph. I'd never seen her so quiet before and it scared me. I racked my brain for something a grown-up might say to patch over the sadness and silence that stretched between us.

"How did you meet? You and Grandad?"

She smiled then and carried on talking to the photograph as she spoke, as if I wasn't there at all. "I was working for the ATA at the time, flying planes from the factories to the RAF squadrons during the war. I'd fly up to six types of planes a day. Hurricanes, Barracudas, Harvards, Wellingtons, Tempests, Spitfires, even Lancaster bombers. We had to fly blind with just maps, a compass, and a watch to help us find our way up and down the country. We didn't have radios back then either – and the weather! Well, it was a miracle that more of the girls didn't end up getting shot down like me…"

"You were shot down?"

She ignored my question and carried on. "…I was delivering a Wellington, I remember. It had been a difficult run, with clouds as thick as porridge over the Shropshire hills. I'd landed safely and switched everything off. Then, I unbuckled my parachute and went down the steps ever so carefully, not wanting to fall over and embarrass myself as there was a big group of pilots on the tarmac having a smoke. I marched over to those lads and asked them where the control room was to get my delivery chitty signed, and do you know what they said?"

I leaned forward and grabbed two biscuits. "What?"

"They said they'd take me over to the control room when the pilot came out of the aeroplane! The cheek!"

I smiled and licked the crumbs from my lips. "What did you do, Granny? Did you wallop them?"

She cackled and coughed, her lungs making that crinkling sound that would become all too familiar to me in the months ahead. "Nope, I just calmly told them I *was* the pilot. Silly twits, they didn't believe me, and all marched off into the aeroplane to try and find the pilot. Well, all except one."

"Grandad?"

"Yes, love. He just laughed at his friends as they went off on a wild goose chase and he showed me where the control room was instead. He said he didn't correct the others with that nonsense about finding the pilot because he wanted to get me to himself. And he did. And that was that."

On her first day at the hospice, me and Mum were

given a whole list of instructions to follow. We weren't allowed to visit when we wanted, only in the registered visiting hours. No more popping in after school or whenever I wanted. We weren't allowed to get Granny too excited – instead we had to keep everything calm and quiet. Speak slowly and in short sentences. Don't rush the conversation. And don't start any of that nonsense about dragons. This last instruction was aimed squarely at me. I did not adhere to it.

"I don't understand why you've put her in there," I said to Mum as we left, making my tone purposefully accusing to get my point across. "They won't let her be herself in there."

"George, don't start. I haven't got the strength for your silly stories. Not today." Mum opened the car door and I got in, crossing my arms and looking resolutely out of the passenger window.

As we pulled away from the hospice, though, I realised I was wrong. The hospice wasn't so bad after all. Because flying into the clouds was a giant red dragon, puffing smoke and looping and rolling as fast as a Supermarine Spitfire.

I opened the car window and waved. Granny waved back and, with a fiery roar, she blew the clouds red, flying further into the sky and out of sight.

On the day of Granny's funeral, I did not cry. There was no need because I knew she hadn't died. Not really.

I was there at the end, holding her hand and staring her square in the eyes. "Granny, what happens to dragons when they die?"

And she chuckled, as best she could through all the tubes. I couldn't quite catch her words, so I removed the oxygen mask and bent over so my ear touched her mouth.

"Us dragons don't die. We just fly somewhere else. Somewhere better."

"Where Grandad is?"

She never answered me, but I knew the answer. She just lay back and smiled, closing her eyes for the last time, lost to other skies where she was flying high with her love ever by her side.

"Daddy, do you have to go away again?" Scarlett asks as I pull on my black boots in the hallway. "I don't like it when you go away for so long."

"Me neither, love, but it's important work that we dragons have to do. Work that keeps you and your sister and mum safe," I say, ruffling my daughter's wild, red hair. The colour skipped two generations from Granny to my youngest. My eldest has her mum's blonde hair and my blue eyes and is nowhere to be seen. "Where's Luna? I've not seen her this morning."

"She's in a grump about you going. Says she's not coming down until you've gone."

I sigh and pull my boots back off, not wanting to get black polish on the upstairs carpet. Luna's bedroom door is shut. I go to knock, but my hand doesn't touch the door before she's yelling at me. "Go away, and I mean it!"

She may not look like her great granny but, my goodness, Luna has inherited her stubborn streak. There were times when she was a tantruming toddler and her mannerisms took me straight back to sitting in my granny's room, watching as the hospice staff tried to calm Granny down during one of her spells.

The same trick worked to settle Luna as it did for Granny. I'd poke a marshmallow on my finger and ask her to toast it. Of course, Granny would just set it alight with her breath and eat it in one mouthful. But little Luna would laugh and laugh, blowing on the marshmallow until it was so covered in her spit that it was a miracle that I then managed to toast the thing with my breath at all. Then she'd take it in her podgy hands and eat that marshmallow in a single gulp, just like her great granny.

This gives me an idea and I run to the kitchen. When I get back, Luna's bedroom door is open, just a crack, but I know better than to barge in.

"Luna, won't you let me in? I've got a marshmallow." I stick the gooey blob on my finger and wiggle it through the gap like some sugary white flag. Then I feel my finger getting warm – hot – as if it's being held under a candle flame. When I pull my hand out, the marshmallow is perfectly toasted.

"There's something I need to tell you, Dad," she says from the other side of the door.

I smile. "What colour are they? The scales?"

I hear her shuffling around on the other side of the door. "Blue."

"Blue? That's the best type, Luna! Blue dragons are the rarest kind and, I would argue, the best kind. They're the best flyers. The ones that'll fly higher than any other sort of dragon you'll find out there."

"As high as you?"

"Higher. There'll be no stopping you, love. Now, how about I take you for one last flight before I head off?" She always loved it when we sailed into the sky, her arms around my neck as she hollered in my ear, demanding more speed and loop-the-loops.

"How about we go together?" She opens the door and stands there, my beautiful daughter with her golden hair, blue eyes, and wings outstretched. I wrap my arms and wings around her, holding her in a tight embrace and stroking the patch of blue on the back of her neck.

"I wish you didn't have to go, Dad," she whispers, pressing her face into my uniform. "If you don't come back, me and Mum and Scarlett won't know what to do without you."

I gulp back the tears. "Me too, love. But there's no need to worry. Remember what I've always told you. Even if I don't come back, I'll still be up there, flying. Somewhere where I can always watch over my girls."

"And with your granny, the dragon?"

"I hope so."

Gemma Church is a former physicist and current science and tech copywriter with a recent Diploma in Creative Writing at Cambridge University. She writes science fiction and fantasy stories and her work has recently appeared in Blackwater Press, Indie Bites and Bag of Bones Press.

Behind You

Kristen Brand

The parking lot was empty when I pulled in, yellow caution tape crisscrossing the trailhead. A big sign reading "Temporarily Closed" covered the maps and information on the wooden notice board, and the whole place looked desolate and ominous.

Or maybe it didn't, and I only thought so because I knew what had happened here.

I parked but didn't get out, my leg twitching as I scanned the trees. It was early morning, the sky gray and the roads foggy as clouds drifted through the mountains. The campers and day trippers wouldn't flood the area for another couple of hours, and the forest was quiet.

A beat-up van pulled into the parking space next to me, and I tensed. A woman got out. She didn't look like a paranormal expert – not that I knew what a paranormal expert was supposed to look like. She wore torn jeans, hiking boots, and a tank top, her only jewelry plain metal bands around her wrists and neck. Tall and well-built, she had dark, messy hair and sleeve tattoos on both arms.

I grabbed my pack and stepped out of the car. "Ms. Romo?"

"Call me Bea," she said. "You must be Dustin."

"Yes, ma'am."

She looked me over, and I could guess what she saw: a burly, bearded man in a park ranger uniform. Hopefully someone who looked trustworthy and not a wacko who'd made the whole thing up.

"Any updates since we talked on the phone?" she asked.

"No, nothing else."

"Then I'll start searching." She strode toward the trailhead. "You can wait here."

I stared at her back for a second, mouth open. That was it? She really didn't waste time on small talk.

"Um." I hurried after her. "I'm going with you."

"You know how to fight monsters?" she asked, not turning around.

"No," I said. "Do *you* know how to navigate the forest, find water, or forage for food?"

She stopped and glowered.

I swallowed. "People die out here, and it's not – it's not always a monster. Most of the time, they just get lost and die from thirst or exposure. I can't handle whatever that thing is out there, but I… I can make sure you get back after you deal with it."

She stared at me for a long moment, her eyes a deep brown. A bird twittered obliviously in a nearby tree, and a car rumbled past on the road. My palms began to sweat, and I didn't know why. I'd hired her to come, found her name on the internet and transferred a down payment despite feeling like a gullible fool. That made me the client. Shouldn't she do as I asked?

But she was the expert. I had no clue what we were dealing with. She did – or at least that's what I desperately hoped.

Finally, she shrugged. "Suit yourself."

She went around the caution tape and started down the trail. After a second's hesitation, I followed.

The air was cool and damp, though it would warm up quickly once the sun cut through the clouds. Leaves rustled overhead in the wind, and the hammering of a woodpecker echoed in the distance. My body felt tauter than a rope bracing a tent pole, and I kept looking over my shoulder. I hated the fear that slithered down my spine. I'd never been afraid of the forest before – cautious and respectful of its dangers, yes, but not afraid.

I stuck close to Bea, but could she keep me safe? She wasn't carrying any weapons. How did she expect to get rid of a monster that had killed two people so far?

"Shouldn't you bring a gun or something?" I asked.

"Not a fan of 'em," she replied. "Why? You carrying?"

"No. I've got bear mace though. You think that'll help?"

"Couldn't hurt."

She was probably just humoring me. I didn't see how bear mace would be any use against that *thing*.

I shuddered. It had been four days since I'd seen it near this very trail. The second person had gone missing that day, a young woman out hiking with friends. She'd been the last one in the group, and one of her friends had turned around to find she simply wasn't there anymore.

I'd joined the search party, hoping she'd simply wandered off the trail and hadn't gone far. When I'd heard a twig snap behind me, I'd turned around…

And seen a monster.

It was taller than me, at least seven feet despite its hunched back. The creature stood on two legs, half hidden behind a tree, and went still when I met its eyes – red eyes glowing in the daylight. It had matted brown fur and a grinning, goatlike face. Curling horns sprouted from its head, and blood stained its fur around a mouth of sharp, jagged teeth.

I'd stumbled back, tripped, and fallen on my ass. When I'd looked back at the tree, the monster had vanished.

Suddenly, losing two hikers on the same trail in a single month had made a lot more sense.

I hadn't told anyone what I'd seen, knowing it would make me look crazy. I'd called in sick the next day, binging beer and ice cream at home in an attempt to forget. It hadn't worked. When I'd heard talk about when to reopen the trail, I'd known I had to do something or more people would die. So I'd scoured the internet and found Beatriz Romo Reyes, freelance exorcist and paranormal consultant.

I hoped she was the real deal. She'd come out here instead of just taking my money, so that was something. But would she really be able to slay the monster?

"This is about where I saw it," I said when we reached a dead tree covered in fungi. "I was off the trail, maybe about ten minutes in that direction." I pointed.

"How far does the trail go?" she asked.

"About a mile further. It ends at an overlook – gorgeous spot. You can see the entire valley. I go there sometimes in the morning when the sun's just coming up. It's tranquil – feels like you're the only person in the world sometimes. No matter what's going on in my life, sitting up there in silence for half an hour makes everything better."

Realizing I was babbling, I snapped my mouth closed.

Bea tilted her head thoughtfully. "Sounds nice."

"It is."

She reached into her pocket and pulled out something that I thought was a necklace at first. Then I realized the chain wasn't looped. A colorless, opaque crystal hung from the bottom of it. Bea gripped the top of the chain, holding it out with the crystal dangling below.

"Um…" I said. "What–"

"Shush."

I shushed. After about ten seconds of the waiting, the crystal began to swing on its chain like a pendulum. Bea looked in the direction it moved, which was pretty much the same direction I'd pointed earlier.

"This way," she said, stuffing the crystal back into her pocket.

I had so many questions.

We hiked off the trail, going slower now that we had to pick our way over uneven ground and through underbrush. Goose bumps spread across my arms, and I couldn't shake the feeling that something was watching us. My imagination or a survival instinct? I didn't know, but I made sure not to lag behind Bea. The last woman who'd gone missing had lagged behind her group, and that's when the monster had gotten her.

My insides went cold as I thought of the dried blood sticking to the messy, matted fur around the creature's mouth. It must have eaten her and the other hiker. I hoped for their sakes that it had been quick.

We kept hiking. I noted the landmarks we passed and checked my GPS frequently. We hadn't been off the trail for long, but you'd be surprised how easy it is to get turned around in the forest. My compass told me we weren't walking in circles, at least. I wondered how far we were from the place where I'd seen the monster. What was the range of its habitat? How far did it travel to hunt? Was it even worth thinking about things like that when it clearly wasn't a normal animal?

"Have you ever seen one of these monsters before?" I asked, huffing a little from exertion.

Bea scanned the forest as she trekked. "Not one exactly like what you described."

"But you know what it is."

Please tell me you know what it is.

She shrugged. "Sometimes things that don't belong in this world find their way here."

I didn't like the sound of that. Or maybe I did. Was it better to think of the creature as some kind of interdimensional demon rather than an undiscovered animal? If it was a native species, did we have any right to get rid of it? It hadn't felt natural when I'd seen it, though. It had felt evil.

Bea stopped, and I was following so closely behind her that I nearly ran into her. Every muscle in my body tensed, and I frantically scanned our surroundings. Had she seen something?

She turned about fifteen degrees and took off at a faster pace. I hurried to keep up, and less than a minute later, we came upon a cave.

It wasn't the type of big, impressive cave that tourists visit. I'd have to crouch to get inside, and the opening wasn't very wide. Surrounded by ferns and tree roots, it would be easy to overlook.

But the smell was hard to miss. It stank of rot, and the buzzing of flies filled the air.

"Stay there," Bea said, and approached it.

I wanted to tell her to stop. Even if this wasn't the monster's lair, there could be a bear or something inside. You can't just waltz into random caves in the wilderness. But I couldn't seem to open my mouth and get the words out.

Bea ducked down, bracing one hand on the mossy rock overhang as she made her way inside. She picked her steps carefully, arm muscles clenching beneath her tattooed skin. How deep did the cave go? What if she didn't come out?

I didn't need to worry, as I never lost sight of her. She stopped partway in, stood there for a second, then spun around and climbed out.

"What?" I asked. "What did you see?"

Her jaw was tight, and the color had drained from her face. "Bones," she said. "Some of them human."

"Old bones?" I asked, voice cracking.

Her head shook jerkily. "Some of them were still juicy."

I swallowed.

Bea rubbed her face. "We'll wait here until it comes back. I doubt we'll be able to take it by surprise, but–"

She jerked up straight and threw a fireball at me.

Yes, an honest-to-God fireball. I couldn't believe it either.

This is it, I thought as the roaring ball of orange flames hurtled toward me. *I'm dead, killed by a shady woman I met on the internet who's apparently pyrokinetic.*

But the fireball soared over my head, singeing the skin on my face, and struck something behind me.

A screech filled the air. I spun around and saw the monster again, the fur on its chest scorched and smoking.

In the back of my mind, deep beneath my panic, I noticed details that I hadn't picked up the last time I'd seen it. Its legs were backwards-jointed and ended in clawed feet. Thicker fur grew on its hunched back, broken twigs and dead leaves tangled up in it. And its limbs looked abnormally long and thin.

It hurled itself at me with a shriek, and I probably would've died if Bea hadn't charged forward and blasted it with fire again.

The flames were so bright that I had to squeeze shut my eyes for a second. When I opened them, bright spots drifting across my vision, the monster had disappeared.

"Shit," Bea hissed, looking left and right.

My chest tightened, and while I didn't quite hyperventilate, my breaths definitely grew faster. I spun around in a circle, searching the trees for the monster. Where had it gone? How could something that big hide so well?

I didn't see anything. I didn't hear anything either, which was weird. No chirping birds. No chittering squirrels. It was like the only animals that dared come near were the flies.

About five feet ahead of me, Bea turned slowly, her fists clenched and stance wide. As soon as she'd turned far enough, the monster edged out from the shadow of a tree behind her.

"Behind you!" I shouted as it rushed her.

She spun. The monster pounced on her, slamming her to the ground. Its teeth went for her throat, but she grabbed its head, arms straining as she pushed it back. Fire flared to life around her hands, searing the fur on its face, but the monster didn't flinch. It pushed through the pain, jaws snapping. It seemed determined to rip out her throat. Bea grunted, arms shaking as its snout pressed slowly closer.

"Hey!"

The monster looked up, and I sprayed bear mace into its eyes.

It shrieked and flailed. Bea kicked it off of her and jumped to her feet. She conjured enough fire to make me scramble back from the heat, and then she shot it all at the monster writhing on the ground.

I cringed from the flames. The heat was painful even several feet away. For the monster, it was lethal.

Its shriek cut off, and the stench of charred flesh hit my nose. I coughed, covering my eyes until the brightness faded and the heat finally cooled. When I could look again, the monster was a blackened corpse, every bit of undergrowth in a five-foot radius of it burnt to a crisp.

Bea sat. Well, honestly it was more like a controlled fall. She was panting, her skin slick with sweat and her jeans dirty.

"Take a deep breath," she said. "Try to calm down."

Calm? I was calm. Then I realized I was babbling, a steady stream of "Holy shit. What happened? How did you do that? Oh my God. What was that thing?" leaving my mouth without my knowledge or permission.

I clenched my jaw shut and focused on breathing for a while.

After a few seconds, I realized the monster's corpse was melting into goop. "What–?" I asked, pointing at it.

Bea stood and dusted off her jeans. "It doesn't belong in this world, remember? It won't leave any remains behind."

So much for calling in scientists to examine the corpse and figure out what the hell that thing had been.

"Come on." She patted me on the shoulder. "Time for you to lead me back to the trail."

I had enough presence of mind to check the GPS before we left. I could lead people back here – leave out the whole monster thing and let them assume a rogue bear or mountain lion was responsible for the killings. At least it would give the families of the missing hikers some closure.

I got us back to the trail, and then Bea took the lead again.

"Wrong way," I said. "Parking lot's in the other direction."

"I know. Let's see this overlook of yours."

We hiked. The sun made its way through the clouds, and as predicted, the day got warmer. I was sweating by the time we reached the top.

The trees parted, revealing a bald spot on the mountain, and a cool wind refreshed my sweaty skin. I walked over to a large rock and sat, resting my elbows on my knees. Bea took a seat beside me.

Blue mountains rose in the distance beneath a pale sky. Verdant forest spread out before us, covering rolling hills. The valley lay below, squares of farmland like patches on a quilt, and a sparkling blue river meandered across the land. The only sound was the wind. A peregrine falcon soared on an updraft ahead, and clouds drifted above, casting shade over us. Tiny wildflowers grew from cracks in the surrounding rocks, and tall grass waved in the breeze.

There were absolutely no monsters here.

"Feel better?" Bea asked.

"A little," I said. "It still doesn't make sense."

"What doesn't?"

"The monster – you shooting fire – nothing that happened makes any sense. It's like some kind of fever dream."

Bea shifted her leg, getting out of the way of some ants marching across the rock. "Did the world really make that much sense before?"

"*Yes*." I paused. "I dunno. Maybe. I'm still freaking out. How are you not freaking out?"

"I do this kind of thing all the time. It's my job."

"Well, it's not mine." I buried my face in my hands. "I'm going to have nightmares for the rest of my life. How do you get over something like that?"

"Try to focus on the positive."

"*What* positive?"

She looked over and smiled. "You saved my life back there. And you called me in the first place, which means that thing will never kill anyone else. You did good, Dustin."

"I guess."

I leaned back and looked out over the valley. It didn't look the same. Would anything look the same after today? Maybe Bea was right, and I should focus on how the monster was dead and I wasn't.

"I need a drink," I said with a groan.

"Great idea." Bea hopped up and headed back to the trail. "You're buying."

Kristen Brand is a speculative fiction author and huge nerd. If you enjoyed Behind You, you'll probably like The Memory of Ghosts, a short story where Bea befriends a ghost she was hired to exorcise.

The True Tale of the Sockburn Worm

Nova Warner

Gulp

Ah, good day there, Charles! I haven't seen you since… Ah yes, that pleasant feast at Hardwick Hall! What a night that was – I swear the lady of the manor was quite the delight. But I digress. What are you doing here? Other than reminiscing about the past with a codger like me, of course. Just here for some drinks with these fine gentlemen? Well, you've chosen a wonderful pub! The pints here are great!

Gulp

What's that? Sockburn? Oh, yes, the beast of Sockburn! Well, if you insist on me retelling that old story, I suppose I'll have to. But I assure you it won't be that different from what those bards say. Actually, there may be a few tiny differences… But the general story will be the same!

Gulp

In fact, I've got a condition. Buy me another drink. Surely I, the grand Sir John Conyers, can't spin the yarn of stories without proper hydration! Aye, just one pint will do, but none of that swill you can get for cheap. Ah yes, this looks good, this'll do. So gentlemen, sitting comfortably? Good, because you better not start shuffling while I'm speaking.

Gulp

Ok. So. You see. After a trip through the exotic lands of Yorkshire I was riding North, back to my family's estate in Sockburn. During my travels I had heard hearsay of a terrifying beast that was stalking the forests of Southern Durham. As any proper knight of honour would, I decided it was my duty to return home and protect it from any such beast, no matter the size of its fangs or the strength of its strikes.

Gulp

After a few days of hard riding, I managed to reach my home in Sockburn. What a pleasant place it is! Have you ever been there, Charles? Oh you should, I do love it so much. The trees are as tall as the barkeep here! And I suspect they're as wide as his wife. And the River Tees runs through the land with a serenity you couldn't find anywhere else! I spent many a night sleeping by it as a young boy. And the– Uh? Of course I'm getting to the point! I'm merely setting the scene as any true storyteller would, you fool! Don't you dare interrupt me again! I've lost my train of thought now. Where was I..?

Gulp

Gah, I'm out now. Another please, barkeep! Ah yes, I remember now! So, I had returned home and headed straight to the tave– No, the church! I believed the reverend would know if the beast was near. Fortunately for all, he did, but unfortunately for those dirty peasa– I mean, hard working local farmers, the beast was merely a long stone's throw away from very church I was standing in. Being the oh-so-honourable knight you all know me as, I kneeled before the altar and prayed to the Grand God for strength and protection. And what a surge I felt! Waves of warmness flowed over me, and I swear I could feel the taste of sweet nectar in my mouth. It was like I was drinking a pint of the finest beer around.

Gulp

Gulp

By God, beer is good. So yes, after I received the strength of God, I strode towards the lair of the beast with confidence only found in men with divine duties – and drunks. I think we all know which of the two I am. In my shining plate armour I must've been a terrifying sight for any vagabond or beast! And what a wondrous weapon I had with me. My trusty falchion – I'm sure you've all heard of it by now. Why, even the dirty hermit over there will have heard of it.

Gulp

It must be the most famous weapon in all the lands! Each Prince-Bishop since that corrupt fool Eadred has blessed it. Oh please don't act outraged, we all know his "deficiencies". He bought his way into office with church funds, hardly very holy of him! What's that, my good fellow? The beast? What beast? Oh yes, the *beast*! I must be dehydrated…

Gulp

Gulp

Gulp

Another please, barkeep! So the beast slammed down to the ground merely feet away from me. With the power of God still flowing through me, I didn't fly off my feet from the impact. And thank the good Lord for that! Somehow the beast rose from the hole it had created and stared me down. What a terrible thing it was! Its skin was covered in orange fur, or was it orange scales? Of course I can tell the difference between the two! But I was slightly too busy to examine the beast's skin. It doesn't matter which one it was, so drop it, ok? Such a rude disruption…

Gulp

Gulp

So we're staring each other down, until suddenly it swung a wing – yes, it had wings – at me! With the agility of a feline, I jumped over the wing and charged towards it. It roared and lashed out with its tail, which I deftly dodged with much ease. God was on my side that day, gentlemen. It only ever managed a single glancing blow upon my plate armour. When I was finally in striking distance, my falchion sliced down upon its devilish face.

Gulp

As I'm sure you can guess, it wasn't very happy with that. Again it swiped at me. But this became its undoing. Rather than knocking me away, it gave me an opening to jump and climb on the wing! With the strength any knight worth his status surely has, I climbed up the beast until I was positioned on top of his head. Falchion in hand, I–

Gulp

–stabbed down and pierced its skull. With a final roar the beast collapsed, its life finally brought to an end. The maiden-in-distress Marie then wrapped her arms around me and exclaimed– What do you mean, who's Marie? Of course I talked about her earlier. Do you think I would really manage to completely miss such a vital character as Marie out of the story? Why, only a fool and drunk could do that, and an honourable knight like I could not possibly be either of those. No, you just haven't been paying attention, you fool. So rude of you.

Now I've lost my train of thought because of you…

Gulp

Gulp

Gulp

Gulp

Two more please, mate, I'm just so thirsty today…

Gulp

Gulp

Gulp

Ah, now I remember where I was. So, the beast is dead by my hands. I stand alone in the clearing. No living soul is in sight. I drop down from the head and wrench the falchion back out. Crimson blood drips from the blade. Just as I start to walk away, a sudden plume of deep black smoke appears in the middle of the clearing. Out steps a lady with piercing orange eyes. Now, while the ordinary man may have been surprised at such an entrance, I am not, due to my status as an honourable knight. She declares herself as Adeliza, a nun. She explains the nature of the beast, and that it was a Wver, or was it a Yvem? Hmm… no, I believe it was a… Wyvern? No, that doesn't sound right. Ah yes, now I remember! It was a worm! Why are you all laughing? Of course I'm aware what a typical worm is. But this was a worm created by the devil! That's why it had wings and a tail!

Gulp

Of course I'm telling the truth! Why would I lie to you fine men? Every single word I uttered was the truth. Yes, I know that the typical man does not have such agility in plate armour, but I am no mere man. I am an honourable knight! Why were there no other such beasts? Why was the body not found by anyone else? There is a very simple explanation for those questions – the devil only made one and he took the body when it was killed–

Gulp

Wait, why are you leaving! Come back! Charles? Charles, please. Don't go, everyone, let's share a drink together. Wait! Screw it, I can drink by myself, then – I don't need any fools like you!

Gulp

Nova Warner is an undergraduate at Durham University studying politics who has recently started to write stories.

Reviews

Editor's Pick

Succulents and Spells by Andi C. Buchanan

The Witchy Fiction author collective is a group of New Zealand authors writing inclusive contemporary fantasy romance novellas – and I love their whole aesthetic! *Succulents and Spells* was the first book of theirs I read, and it turned out to be exactly as delightful as I'd hoped. The main character, Laurel, is a witch from a highly talented magical family, who is struggling to find the niche her magic fits into, so for now she's dabbling in herbalism and hedgewitchery while battling feelings of incompetence. When monster researcher Marigold comes to ask for some samples from Alfred (the pink and yellow monster that lives in the shadows in Laurel's flat), Laurel is dragged into two things: a magical mystery that could unlock the secret to her power, and a flirtation that could turn into something more…

This f/f romance is *so* sweet. I loved both Laurel and Marigold, and thought that their scenes together were adorable. This is very much the beginning of a relationship, and is totally PG in terms of the romance, but even though I usually prefer a little more heat, it still feels completely fulfilling and enjoyable! The characterisation is really elegantly done and makes it easy to root for both women to succeed in their goals *and* get together. Laurel's frustration with her magic will ring true for anyone who's made it out into the world and then thought 'well, now what?'. Marigold is autistic, and though she's upfront about expecting this to be an issue in her relationship with Laurel, it never is – I thought the subject was handled really sensitively, as you'd expect from an author who is neurodivergent themself. Both Marigold and Laurel bring a lot of preconceptions about themselves to their relationship, and watching them support each other to relax into themselves is lovely – I'd love to see more books like this, with strong, supportive f/f relationships!

Though this is only a novella, it throws open so many options for further books in the series, and I'll definitely be reading anything else in this world, whether it continues to focus on Marigold and Laurel, or spins off to look at some of the other characters. I'm intrigued to know more about Marigold's research into monster genetics, for sure, even if it's just in the background! The monsters are so fascinating (especially the wonderful Alfred!) and the mixture of magic and science really made this stand out for me as an interesting setting. I thought this was a great light-hearted take on the urban fantasy genre – and the New Zealand setting shines, making it very different from another dark magical London or New York. Though there's plenty of magic and peril, this is a fairly slice-of-life-y book, which is something I love. It would actually be great for those who loved the *Tea Dragon Society* books, but want a prose book instead of a graphic novel!

If you're in the mood for a bit of escapism, this is going to be perfect for you. It's an utterly adorable read, as fluffy as one of the monsters in it, and I'm looking forward to future books in the *Windflower* series.

About the author: *Andi C. Buchanan lives among streams and faultlines just north of Wellington, Aotearoa New Zealand. Their forthcoming novel Sanctuary is about found family and haunted houses. Winner of a Sir Julius Vogel Award, their genre-blending novella "From a Shadow Grave" explores a historical murder, the legends surrounding it, and what might have been. Andi's short fiction has previously been published in Fireside, Cossmass Infinities, Apex, and more. When not writing they enjoy cheese, knitting,*

and winning disputes with the neighbour's cat.

About the reviewer: Asha is the Indie Bites Review Editor. She is also a book blogger with a life-long love of fantasy and a towering TBR.

A Fate of Wrath and Flame by K.A. Tucker

Review by Rosina from Lace and Dagger Books

A Fate Of Wrath and Flame is a new adult fantasy romance novel by K.A. Tucker, who may be better known for her contemporary romance. This book follows Romeria, a gifted thief who has been living on the streets since she was a teen. On a job one night, she runs into a mysterious woman who tells her she has a job for her. Not wanting to take it on but not having a choice, Romeria goes along with her. The mission turns out to be in another world on the verge of war and filled with elemental magic. Romeria's quest should be simple: she has to steal a stone from a sacred garden. But the identity she has assumed turns out to be that of a captured princess, an enemy who had just poisoned the previous king and queen –not to mention, the fiancée of the new king. Romeria winds up pulled into a scheme by the king, but that's fine by her. It might just allow her to complete her mission.

The first thing I obviously have to talk about is romance. In Zander's mind, this is a second-chance romance. But as a reader, we know that this Romeria is different. You understand why Zander doesn't want to trust her. You get why none of the characters trusts her, actually. But Romeria is also having to come to terms with this identity. This world is different, and the real princess committed some horrific crimes. Due to these reasons, the romance is obviously a bit of a slow burn. They are attracted to each other pretty early on, but some things put Romeria off Zander at first. He has secrets from her, things that wouldn't be a secret to anyone from their world, and it makes things strained. But that was also what made it kind of interesting. It's hate-to-love but not necessarily in a way you usually expect to see. The hate is somewhat due to the way he treated her. But also due to things he can't change. Things she learns to accept because it's just down to differences in their worlds. I quite liked that, as it meant that there was some character growth.

With this book going from our world to another, world-building was important. With Tucker mostly being a contemporary romance author, you wouldn't assume that world-building is her strong point – but she did a great job in this one. This is a world with multiple species, countries and people, all unlike our own. Their customs are different, and though there are some that Romeria understandably can't abide by, a lot of it she comes to accept. The things she doesn't like? Xander and many others aren't fans of either and wish to change. I will note that many of these issues do relate to slavery and even sex trafficking, so if that's something you're not comfortable reading, this won't be the book for you. Tucker does it in a way that you feel for those characters, and like Romeria, you want to see changes made.

Romeria is someone poor and out on the street. She knows what it's like to have nothing, but now she's instantly been elevated to have everything. We know this will make her a good queen, and it was wonderful to see her coming into that role. Yes, technically, it's a role that belongs to someone else. But that's also why you know she'll do a great job of it.

The other fantasy elements of this plot lead to plenty of court intrigue and interesting magic. The characters are mostly elementals, but seers and healers are featured too. The magic system is somewhat limited with the possibility of powerful characters. You get plenty of information regarding the magic, as Romeria needs to learn, but I definitely want to learn more. And I'm pretty sure we'll be getting that in book two…

If you're looking for a fantasy romance with monster elements, then this is one for you. I can't go into too much detail because of spoilers, but the gods of this world have created monsters. You'll come across demon-like monsters that hunt humans. You'll also see some more human-looking monsters that you might not quite be expecting – I know I wasn't! I enjoyed the twists and the backstory behind these elements, and I think it was really well done. These monster elements impact the path Romeria chooses, as well as the romance itself. This book has been compared to *From Blood and Ash*, and with these elements, I can see why. But I think that perhaps *A Fate of Wrath and Flame* was more to my preference.

I listened to this book in audio and I will admit that even though it's not that long, it did take me over a week to get through. Usually, I'd say that's a bad thing, but it actually worked in this book's favour. I was able to slow down and really enjoy the book rather than feeling like I wanted to finish it as soon as possible. I was able to stop listening for a few days, yet when I picked the book back up? I wasn't at all lost, and I didn't need to go back at all. This was a book I could dip in and out of.

After finishing the first one, I want to continue with this series. The second book is out in July 2022, so it's one I'm going to think about putting on preorder. And even if I don't? I'll definitely be reading it at some point. After the ending, I'm curious as to where the magical elements and plot are going to go. I also want to see how the romance develops now that Romeria's secret has been revealed.

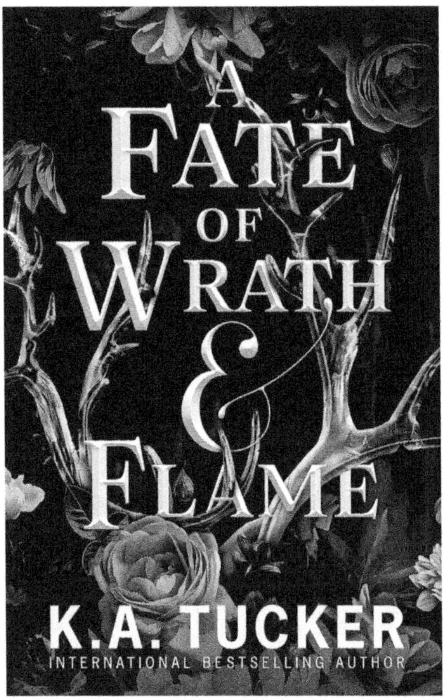

About the author: K.A. Tucker writes captivating stories with an edge. She is the international bestselling author of over twenty novels. Her books have been featured in national publications including USA Today, Globe & Mail, Suspense Magazine, Publisher's Weekly, Oprah Mag, and First for Women. She has been nominated for the Goodreads Choice Award for Best Romance 2013 for Ten Tiny Breaths and Best Romance 2018 for The Simple Wild. Keep Her Safe made Suspense Magazine's Best of 2018 list for Romantic Suspense. K.A. Tucker currently resides in a quaint town outside of Toronto.

About the reviewer: Rosina is a long-time fantasy reader who revels in the queer and dark. She/they.

Printed in Great Britain
by Amazon

80113725R00068